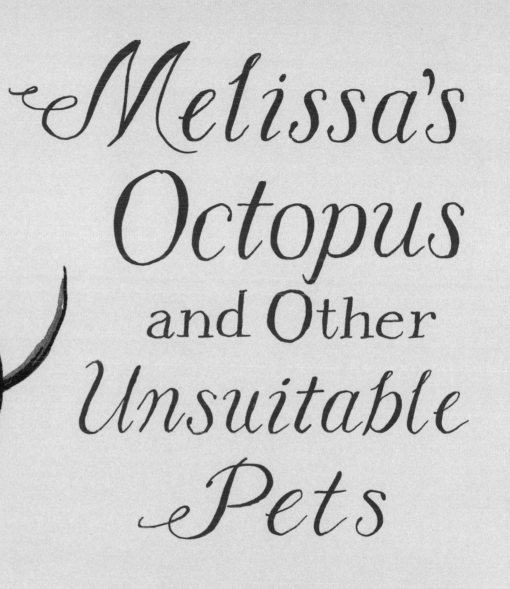

Melissa's Octopus
and Other
Unsuitable
Pets

CHARLOTTE VOAKE

CANDLEWICK PRESS

Here is Melissa's octopus.

What a splendid creature he is.

Unfortunately, an octopus is not a very suitable pet.

You should see the mess he makes in the bathroom!

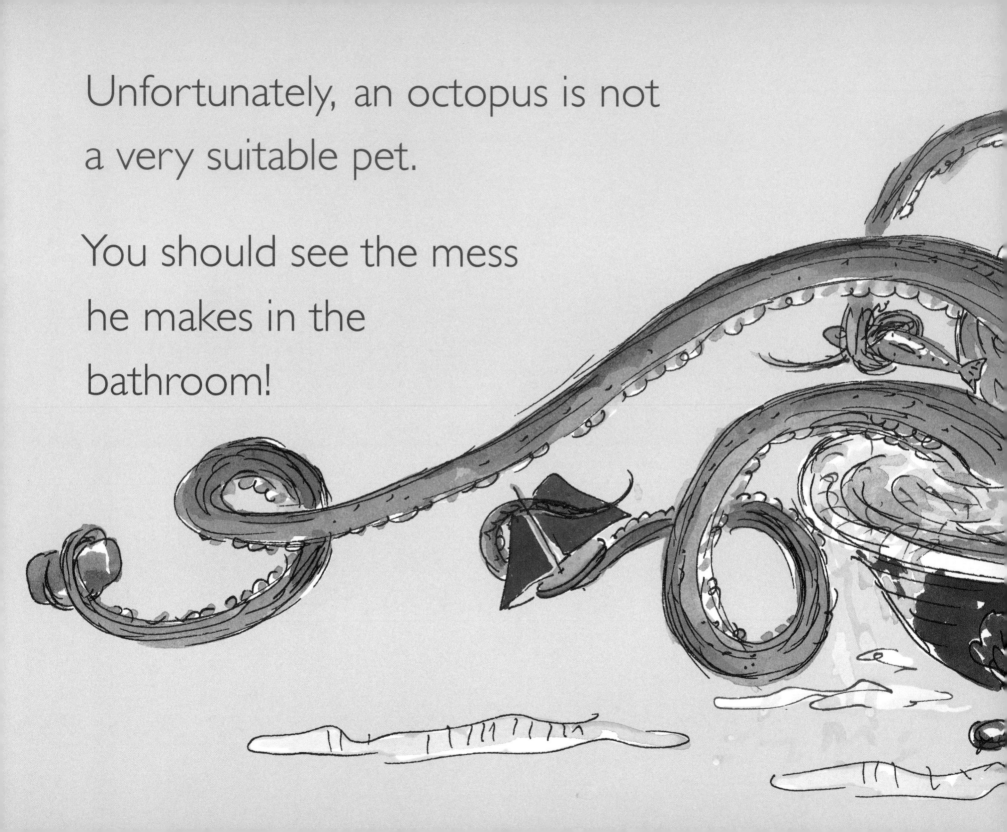

Thomas has a much
smaller pet—
a lovely little mole.
But the mole is always
digging tunnels,
which makes him
very hard to find.

Thomas never knows
where he'll pop up next.

Poor Betty!

She can never find her pet, either.

He's a chameleon.

Where can he be today?

This is Arthur's warthog.

Isn't he a beautiful animal!

But a warthog is not a great pet.
A warthog does exactly what it wants.

Caroline's giraffe is a gentle pet
with lovely long legs.

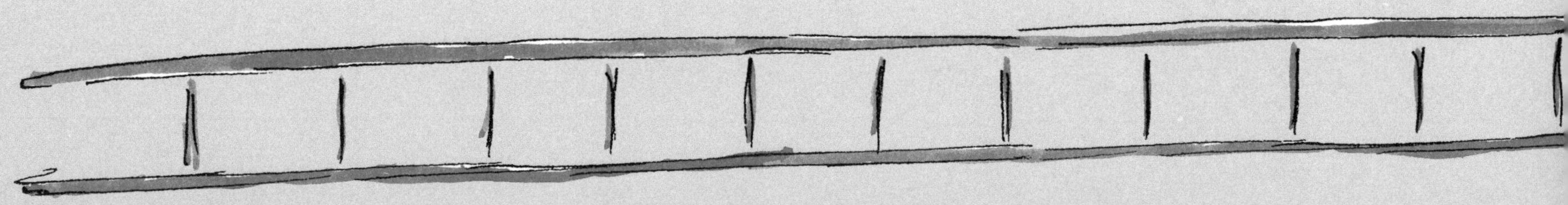

But she's a bit too tall for Caroline.

This is Simon's worm.

He's not a bad pet, but Simon never
knows which end to talk to.

This is Peter's elephant.
He is very big.

He is also VERY heavy.

Sometimes he's upstairs . . .

and he ends up downstairs by mistake.

Kevin and Bertrand
are very proud of their new pet crocodile.
They have invited Melissa, Thomas, Betty, Arthur,
Caroline, Simon, and Peter over to see it.
Look at its glittering teeth!

HEY, CROCODILE!
WHAT HAVE YOU DONE
WITH KEVIN AND
BERTRAND?

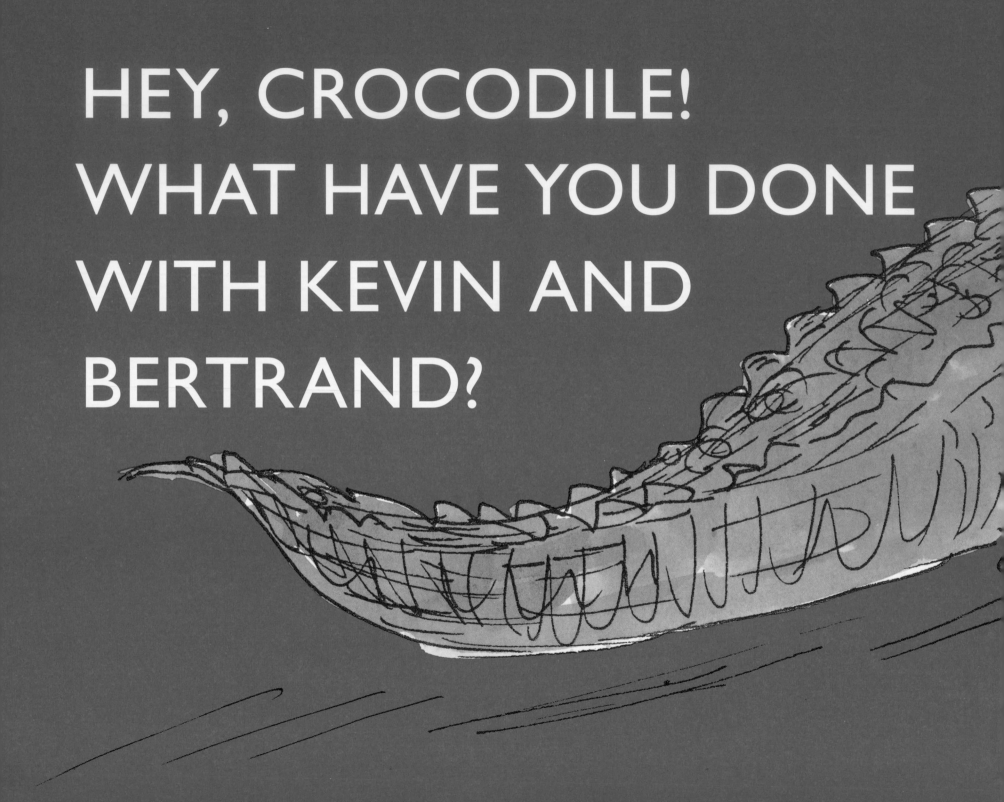

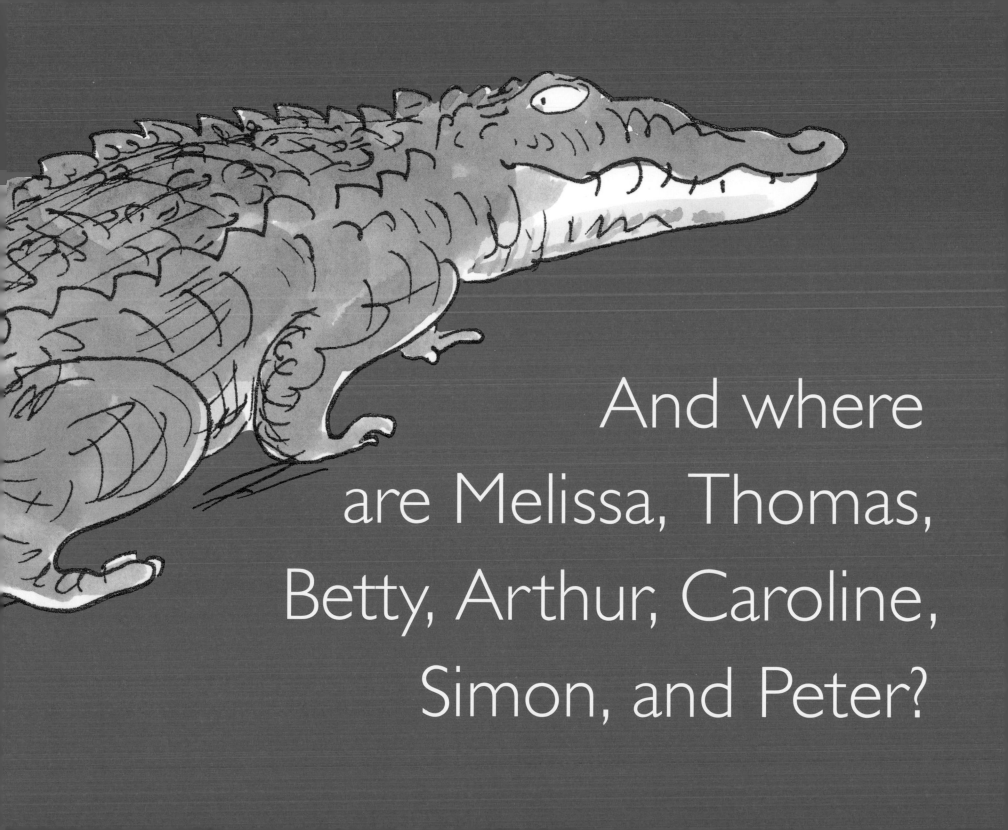

And where are Melissa, Thomas, Betty, Arthur, Caroline, Simon, and Peter?

Phew!

They're all having
a snack.

But next time, they'd
better watch out. . . .

A crocodile really is . . .

the MOST UNSUITABLE
PET OF ALL!

To my
beautiful
badly behaved
pet parrot,
Gwen

Copyright © 2014 by Charlotte Voake. All rights reserved. No part of this book may be reproduced, transmitted, or stored in an information retrieval system in any form or by any means, graphic, electronic, or mechanical, including photocopying, taping, and recording, without prior written permission from the publisher. First U.S. edition 2015. Library of Congress Catalog Card Number 2013957483. ISBN 978-0-7636-7481-6. This book was typeset in Gill Sans. The illustrations were done in pen and watercolor. Candlewick Press, 99 Dover Street, Somerville, Massachusetts 02144. visit us at www.candlewick.com.
Printed in Shenzhen, Guangdong, China. 15 16 17 18 19 20 CCP 10 9 8 7 6 5 4 3 2 1